What-a-Mess is hungry. Extremely hungry. The family have decided that he is getting too fat and have reduced the size of his meals. To make things worse, they have stopped his daily bowl of milk, too. What-a-Mess needs a real brainwave if he is to solve this food shortage...

From the ITV series produced by Bevanfield Films for Central Independent Television
Adapted for television by Tim Forder
Illustrations by Nigel Alexander, Primary Design
Licensed by Link Licensing

British Library Cataloguing in Publication Data
Muir, Frank, *1920-*
    What-a-Mess has a brainwave.
    I. Title   II. Wright, Joseph, *1947-*
    823'.914[J]
    ISBN 0-7214-1418-4

First edition

Published by Ladybird Books Ltd Loughborough Leicestershire UK
Ladybird Books Inc Auburn Maine 04210 USA

© Central Independent Television plc/What-a-Mess Ltd MCMXC
© In presentation LADYBIRD BOOKS LTD MCMXCI

Printed in England (3)

FRANK MUIR'S

What-a-Mess
has a
Brainwave

Based on Frank Muir's original concept and story, and Joseph Wright's illustrations

Ladybird Books

It was a beautiful sunny morning. Small creatures mucked about on the grass and birds twittered in the treetops. Everyone seemed to be enjoying themselves.

Everyone that is, except What-a-Mess, the fat and rather smelly Afghan puppy of royal descent, who was having a Very Serious Think.

He was having it in his Very Serious Thinking Place – a dustbin by the old barn.

Unfortunately, because What-a-Mess was rather fat, and the dustbin was rather small and full of kitchen rubbish, the puppy had trouble squashing into it.

But it was warm and friendly in there, with interesting smells, so it was the perfect place for a puppy with some Serious Thinking to do.

The only problem was that it was so cosy that every time he tried to think seriously, he dozed off, and when he woke up he'd forgotten what he was supposed to be thinking about.

In search of inspiration, he trotted back to the house to get something to eat. It was nearly half an hour since breakfast and his tummy was beginning to make peculiar grunting noises.

He made his way towards the kitchen forgetting, as he always did, to remove the dustbin lid. Suddenly, as the puppy's tiny little brain cleared, he remembered what he had gone to his Serious Thinking Place to think seriously about.

It was how to get the humans in the house to give him back his daily bowl of milk.

What-a-Mess didn't like milk very much. But when the humans started giving him a bowl of it as a treat, his friends – the cat-next-door and Cynthia the hedgehog – were delighted.

Then tragedy struck. The puppy's milk was stopped. It had happened the day before, when What-a-Mess was wondering whether the floor in the sitting room was as slippery as the floor in the hall.

To discover the answer to this tricky question, What-a-Mess had run along the passage and launched himself at speed through the sitting room door.

The sitting room floor *was* as slippery as the hall. The vicar's wife was just sitting down on her chair for tea with the family at the time. What-a-Mess skidded along the floor and whipped her chair from under her.

The man of the house was not amused. As a punishment he had declared that What-a-Mess was to have his bowl of milk stopped.

When What-a-Mess arrived in the kitchen, he found that the family had gone out.

There, in front of him, was the empty milk bowl. And since he had already eaten all his breakfast he suddenly felt hungrier than ever.

What-a-Mess was used to four square meals a day, with a light snack every half hour or so in between. But the family had recently become worried that he was growing rather fat and had reduced his portions, so What-a-Mess was feeling even more ravenous than usual.

What-a-Mess searched through the refrigerator in vain. There wasn't so much as a leftover biscuit or sausage. And there was no milk for his friends.

He went into the living room. He thought he might manage to keep going for a bit on a silk, hand-embroidered cushion cover, while he thought about how to get his milk back.

But it merely seemed to get him more in the mood for a slap-up, early-mid-morning-get-me-through-till-elevenses nibble.

Then he tried upstairs. He rummaged around in the bathroom. There were all the usual things, like a tube of stuff smelling of peppermint, which he bit into, and a roll of pink paper, which he tried to eat, but which kept rolling away from him – like he had seen it do on the television.

By this time What-a-Mess was feeling really miserable. He decided to go to his Second Favourite Hiding Place, under the stairs, where he could sulk in peace.

He was soon joined by the cat-next-door, who quickly noticed that something was wrong.

'What's the matter with you, then?' she purred.

'I'm hungry!' snapped What-a-Mess.

'Hungry?' said the cat. 'You're always hungry.'

'Not always,' said What-a-Mess. 'It's mainly when I'm trying to do some Serious Thinking.'

'What have *you* got to think about?' asked the cat-next-door in a rather unpleasant way.

So What-a-Mess explained that his milk had been stopped and his food portions had been reduced.

'Why don't you please the family by performing some very kind deed?' said the cat-next-door. 'Then they might give you more to eat.'

It was at that moment that What-a-Mess had a brainwave.

It wasn't much of a brainwave really, but to What-a-Mess, who had never had a brainwave before, it was a very important event indeed.

He knew then and there exactly what he would do for the family. They had always made meals for him, so, in return, he would make a meal for them!

He was determined that this should be a very special meal.

He knew that there was nothing edible in the house, but he had often seen the man digging up plants in the garden, which the family had then eaten.

Digging came naturally to What-a-Mess and he had soon gathered a blue lupin, a geranium and a small rhododendron, which all seemed much more colourful than the miserable green stuff the family usually ate.

He dragged the plants back to the house and took them into the kitchen.

Then What-a-Mess added some salad dressing. The nearest thing he could find was some engine oil from the garage.

What-a-Mess had often seen flour being used in cooking, but he couldn't find any in the kitchen.

Then he remembered having seen something very similar in the bathroom, which, anyway, had a much more interesting smell than the flour the family normally used. What-a-Mess mixed up the concoction by jumping up and down on it.

By the time the family returned, What-a-Mess had completely tired himself out and had fallen asleep in his basket with a teatowel over his head.

In his sleepy state, he hardly heard the gasps of horror as the family discovered the mess in the kitchen.

But he *did* hear the woman say, 'Just look at our poor little puppy. He's so hungry because we took his milk away that he's tried to eat the garden flowers.

'From now on, puppy,' the woman went on, 'You shall have as much milk as you want and we will give you larger portions of food every meal time.'

With these happy words ringing in his ears, What-a-Mess closed his eyes and drifted gently back to sleep.